AUBREY'S FITNESS KIDS

Written by: Heddrick McBride and Aubrey Brown

Illustrated by: HH-Pax

Edited by: Yolonda D. Coleman

ISBN-10:1482662086
ISBN-13:978-1482662085

DEDICATION

Eating well and staying healthy are important. Aubrey's Fitness Kids was written to provide children with options for healthy living. We are aware that child obesity is on the rise and is linked to diabetes, high blood pressure, and depression. The goal of Aubrey's Fitness Kids is to make eating right and exercise a fun family activity.

This book is dedicated to my children, Tatiana, AJ, and Ariana, who are my heart and soul! I also want to thank my family and friends, especially my wife. You give me the support I need to continue reaching my goals.

Grocery Shopping

Family, let's get out of the car. We are about to feel wealthy.
Once we finish shopping for the right foods we'll be healthy.

Son, let's find some whole grain we can eat.

Great job! You found the bread made of wheat.

We chose apples, bananas, oranges, and pears.
We found some tasty fruit. I'm glad they were there.

Great job, guys, we like what we see.
I can tell this family is healthy as can be.

We found carrots, corn, and broccoli, all of our favorite veggies. We even grabbed some lettuce for a meal that's not too heavy. We grabbed low fat milk and light cheese, so we can have some dairy. We also grabbed a snack for the tooth fairy.

Family, I am proud of the food we picked to eat. We did so well, that we can finally have our favorite treat.

ICE CREAM!

By telling time we can see when and where our meals should be. Following a watch or clock we can make our hunger stop.

Here is a list of the different meals of the day along with different meal choices. There is also a clock and a watch to tell us what time we should be eating these meals.

Breakfast (morning 7am-11am)

Common Choices

- Whole grain cereal
- Scrambled eggs
- Whole grain pancakes
- Whole grain waffles
- Turkey bacon
- Oatmeal
- Baked potatoes
- Granola
- Breakfast burrito
- Whole grain and fruit muffins
- Yogurt
- Fruit
- Apple juice
- Cranberry juice
- Orange juice
- Tea
- Hot chocolate
- Water
- Low-fat milk

Lunch (afternoon 11am-2pm)

Common Choices

- Sandwich (lean cold cut, peanut butter and jelly, cheese)
- Fruit
- Mini pizza roll with whole wheat tortilla
- Chicken salad
- Egg salad
- Granola
- Grilled chicken
- Grilled salmon
- Vegetables
- Tuna fish
- Whole wheat wrap
- Barbecue chicken sandwich with whole wheat bun
- Low-fat milk
- Water
- Fruit Juice

Snack (late afternoon 2pm-4pm)

Common Choices

- Fruit
- Cereal
- Peanut butter
- Low-fat potato chips
- Apple sauce
- Cheese
- Trail mix
- Popcorn
- Crackers
- Water
- Fruit juice
- Low-fat milk

Dinner (6p-8pm)

Common Choices

- Chicken

- Turkey chops

- Spaghetti and meatballs

- Macaroni and cheese

- Vegetables

- Fish

- Turkey

- Rice

- Baked potatoes

- Fruit

- Salad

- Water

- Juice

Dessert (after dinner 7pm-9pm)

Common Choices

- Low-fat ice cream

- Fruit parfaits

- Whole wheat carrot cake

- Fruit

- Hot chocolate

- Baked apples

- Crackers

- Low-fat chocolate cookies

- Juice

- Water

Now we will always know when it is TIME TO EAT!

Before you can be strong and perform your best,
you have to pass Aubrey's fitness test.

It starts with stretching; you must try to touch your toes.

The harder you try the farther your body goes.

Then do some jumping jacks to keep the body loose.
You have to be flexible so you won't have an excuse.

Then try some push ups where you lift your own weight. At first it's tough, but later your arms and chest will look great.

Next, go running for a long distance.

You can go as far as you like without any resistance.

In the middle of this test you must stay healthy and be smarter.
Remember to take quick breaks and drink cold water.

The final part of the test is most important. Always play fair and be a good sportsman. Never cheat to win the game or to be the best. Give your all at what you do. You passed Aubrey's fitness test!

Aubrey's Tips

Best snacks for kids:

- Apple sauce
- Peanut butter
- Smoothies
- Cereal
- Fruit
- Trail mix
- Cheese
- Popcorn

Best foods for kids:

- Milk
- Apples
- Peanut butter
- Yogurt
- Tuna fish
- Breakfast cereal
- Eggs
- Vegetables
- Oatmeal
- Sunflower seeds

Worst foods:

- Soda
- Hamburgers
- Hot dogs
- Ice cream
- Bologna
- Whole milk
- American cheese
- French toast and tater tots
- Pizza with meat on it
- Chocolate bars

Health tips:

- Take family outings such as hiking, swimming, bicycling and playing in the park.

- Make sure children do at least 20 minutes of physical activity every day.

- Eat a fruit or vegetable with each meal.

- Drink at least 5 glasses of water daily.

Workout exercises (fun stuff):

- Running in place

- Jumping Jacks

- Jump Rope

- Jogging

- Push ups

- Crunches/Sit ups

- Squats

- Skipping

- Dancing

Visit www.mcbridestories.com for more titles.